OH WHERE, OH WHERE COULD THAT SILLY DOG BE?

This book is a work of fiction. The names, characters and events in this book are the products of the author's imagination or are used fictitiously. Any similarity to real persons living or dead is coincidental and not intended by the author.

Oh Where, Oh Where Could That Silly Dog Be?

Copyright © 2021 by Chris, Amanda, and Noah Wirth

All rights reserved. Neither this book, nor any parts within it may be sold or reproduced in any form or by any electronic or mechanical means, including information storage and retrieval systems, without permission in writing from the author. The only exception is by a reviewer, who may quote short excerpts in a review.

Library of Congress Control Number: 2021936095

ISBN (hardcover): 9781662912290

ISBN (paperback): 9781662912306

eISBN: 9781662912313

OH WHERE, OH WHERE COULD THAT SILLY DOG BE?

Chris, Amanda, and Noah Wirth

Silly Dog Media

Did she climb to the top of a silly dog tree?

Oh where, oh where did that silly dog go?

Did she get buried below a pile of silly dog snow?

Oh where, oh where did that silly dog stray?

Did she fall fast asleep on the silly dog hay?

Did she chase a round tire away
from her silly dog home?

Did she chase rabbits and squirrels through the silly dog park?

Did she get silly dog directions from a gnome that could talk?

Oh where, oh where did that silly dog race?

Did she build a silly dog rocket
and launch into space?

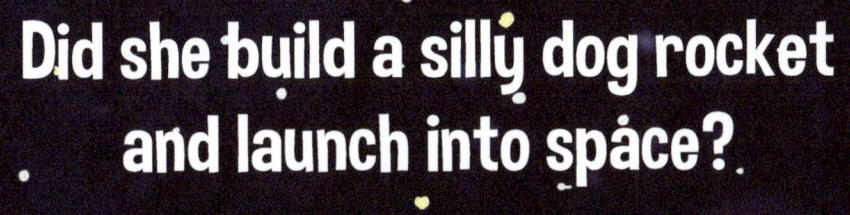

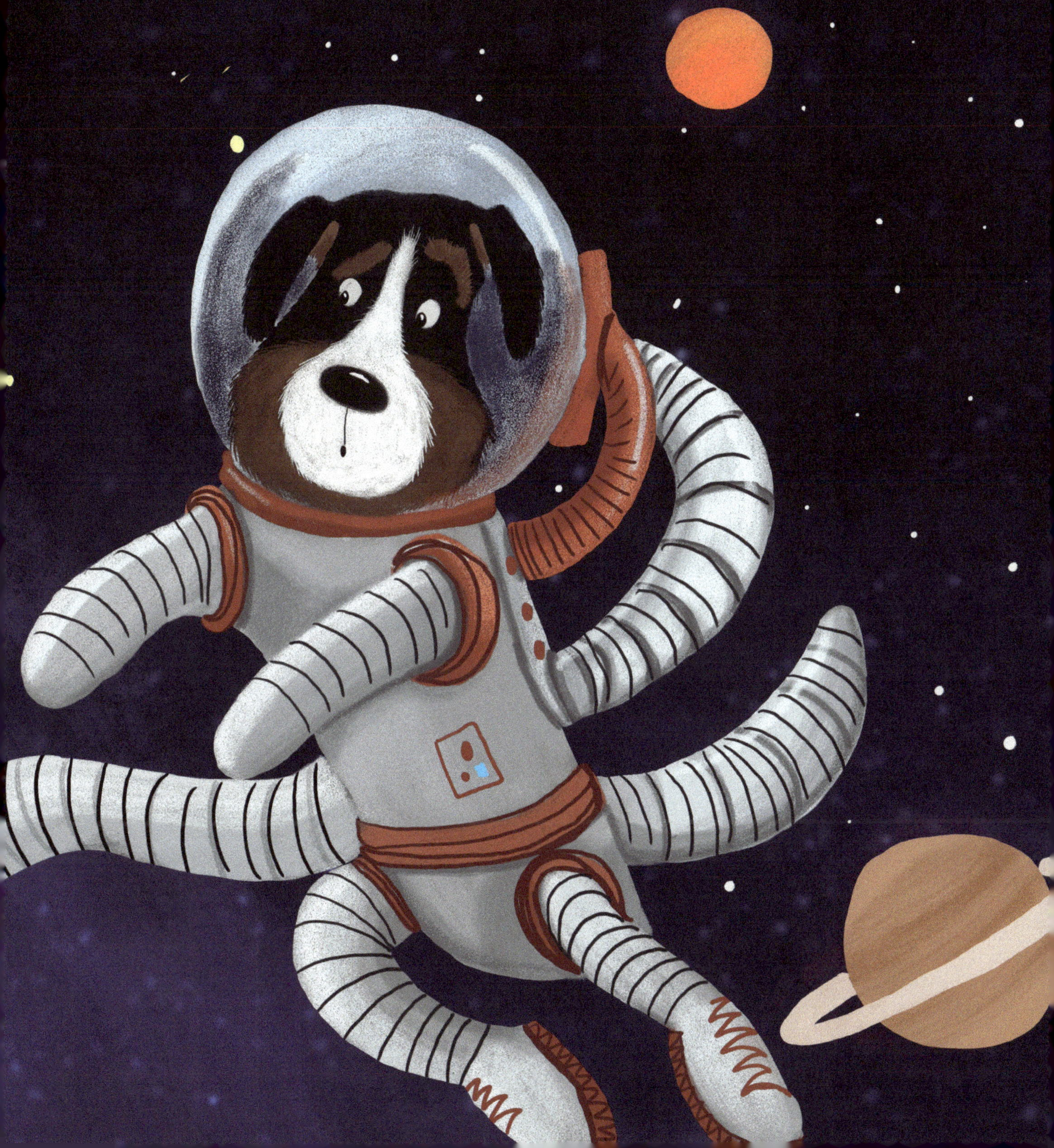

Oh where, oh where did that silly dog jog?

Did she hide within a hollow silly dog log?

Oh where, oh where did that silly dog skip?

Oh there, oh there is where silly dog's nose led . . .

She was chasing imaginary monsters under my bed.

Authors: Chris, Amanda, and Noah Wirth live in Michigan with the original Silly Dog: Reese, their Greater Swiss Mountain Dog. The newest human puppy, Tilly, joined the pack in 2019. The Wirths imagined all of the places their silly dog might be one day while she was not where she was supposed to be. Noah finished the book in fourth grade. He enjoys science, reading, soccer, swimming, playing with his friends, and of course, adventures with his silly dog! Chris and Amanda are both attorneys who enjoy travel and supporting the dreams of their children.

Illustrator: Helena Crevel is a children's book illustrator working in traditional and digital techniques from her home studio in Paris, France. She enjoys illustrating stories about animals and nature, dogs being among her favorites. In her free time, she enjoys traveling the world, organizing creative workshops for children and gardening.

The Wirths collaborated with Helena during the COVID-19 Pandemic lockdowns. The international exchange was a productive outlet and fun way to connect during a time when connecting looked a little different.

CPSIA information can be obtained
at www.ICGtesting.com
Printed in the USA
BVHW020348220521
607795BV00007B/1491